Jane Goodall
A GOOD AND TRUE HEART

Written by Ann Martin Bowler

STECK-VAUGHN

A Harcourt Company

www.steck-vaughn.com

CONTENTS

Introduction

Hiking through a wild forest in Africa, Jane Goodall followed a chimpanzee she'd named David Graybeard. He swung from tree to tree over her head. Then Jane became tangled in vines and was sure she had lost the chimp. When she came to a clearing in the forest, she was surprised to see David again. He was sitting by the edge of a stream and seemed to be waiting for her.

Jane slowly sat down next to David. She noticed that David's eyes looked soft and peaceful. David sat still and calmly looked at Jane. Jane saw a piece of fruit lying on the ground, and she offered it to David. He took the fruit but dropped it quickly. He surprised Jane by holding her hand for a few seconds. The two of them sat near each other for a long while. Then David got up and wandered off into the forest. Jane was deeply moved and wanted to remember this moment forever.

She began to feel she had found the place where she belonged. She also began to feel she had found what she came into the world to do.

David Graybeard

CHAPTER 1

Dreams of Africa

Jane Goodall was born in London, England, in 1934. She lived there with her parents, her younger sister, Judy, and a dog named Peggy.

Animals always interested Jane. When she was four years old, she began to wonder how eggs came out of chickens. One day she decided to find out. For almost four hours, she sat silently on the itchy straw in a henhouse. Jane was delighted when she finally saw the egg drop out of the hen. She ran to tell her mother what she had seen. Jane had no idea that her family had been searching for her everywhere. They had even called the police.

However, her mother was not angry. "How lucky it was that I had an **understanding** mother!" Jane says. "Instead of being angry because I had given her a scare, she wanted to know the wonderful thing I had just seen."

When Jane was very young, her father gave her a stuffed chimpanzee named Jubilee. This toy was named after a chimp at the London Zoo. Jane still has that stuffed animal today.

Jane with Jubilee

World War II broke out in 1939 when Jane was five. The war had many effects on her and her family. Her father joined the British Army and was away from home for many years. Jane, her mother, and her sister went to live with Jane's grandmother in a house they called the Birches. This big house in the country had belonged to Jane's family for many years. Her parents felt that their family would be safe there because it was far from any city.

Jane's family had little money during the war, so she learned to be **thrifty**. She learned that doing simple things could be fun. One of the things that Jane enjoyed was reading. She often used a flashlight to read in bed long after her mother had turned out her light.

The Story of Doctor Dolittle was Jane's favorite book. In this story an animal doctor tries to help monkeys in Africa. For Jane, the best part of the story was that Dr. Dolittle could talk to animals. Jane's parents could not afford to buy books, so Jane read the library's copy again and again. She was thrilled when her grandmother gave her a copy of her own one day. She also loved *The Jungle Book,* a lively tale about jungle animals. Because she loved stories about animals, Jane began to dream about working with them.

When she was a girl, Jane formed a nature club with her sister and two girls who lived nearby. They called it the Alligator Club. Jane was the club's leader. The girls went on nature hikes and had snail races. They camped in an overgrown part of Jane's backyard.

Jane with her father, mother, and sister

The Alligator Club also collected flowers, bones, and seashells. They set up their collections and made a museum. The girls invited people to take a look at their museum. Then they asked their visitors for **donations**. The donations went to a group that cared for old horses.

Jane **excelled** in school, especially in the subjects that she enjoyed. But she was the happiest on weekends and holidays. She loved to spend whole days outdoors playing with her pets, especially her dog Rusty. Rusty had joined Jane's family after they moved to the Birches. Rusty became Jane's favorite pet, and she taught him all kinds of tricks. She taught him to jump through a hoop and to climb a ladder.

Jane learned a lot by working with Rusty. She saw that if she petted Rusty and talked softly to him, he learned quickly. If she became angry with him, he would not do anything that she asked.

Jane with Rusty

By the time Jane was 18, she was **determined** to go to Africa to work with animals. However, her family did not have the money to send her. Her mother suggested that Jane train to be a secretary. Jane moved to London to do her training there.

In her first job as a secretary, Jane worked in a medical clinic. This job taught Jane to be **grateful** for her health. Ever since that time, Jane has felt a special closeness to people who are sick or disabled, and she tries to treat them with **compassion**.

During another early job, Jane lived with her father in London. Her parents had divorced when Jane was 12. She was happy to spend time with her father. While she lived in London, Jane often went to the London Zoo. Back then zoo animals often lived in small concrete cages. Seeing the animals in the cages made Jane sad. She promised herself that one day she would help animals in zoos have better lives.

Jane was a happy young woman, but she never forgot her dream of going to Africa. Every day she wondered when she would be able to go. Every day she dreamed about what she would do when she finally got there.

CHAPTER 2

To Africa

One day Jane received a letter from an old school friend, Clo Mange. Clo invited Jane to come to Africa and stay at her family's farm in Kenya. Jane was overjoyed! She wanted to get to Africa as soon as possible. Jane quit her job in London and went home to the Birches. Jane's mother would not let her go to Africa unless she also had a ticket home. Jane went to work as a waitress in a big hotel near her family's home. She saved enough money to buy a round-trip boat ticket to Africa.

Jane Goodall was 23 years old when she sailed for Africa. She found it hard to believe that her dream was finally coming true! During the 21-day voyage, she sat on the deck of the ship for hours. She studied the ocean and its animals. She spotted dolphins, flying fish, and sharks. She was excited to make friends with the other travelers.

Jane stayed with Clo for three weeks at the Mange family's farm. Because Jane had been taught to be **independent**, she knew she could not stay with them forever. She soon left the farm and went to work at a rather dull job. However, she kept her eyes and ears open. She hoped that she would soon be working with African animals. Soon someone learned of Jane's interest in animals and suggested that she go to see Dr. Louis Leakey. Dr. Leakey and his wife, Mary, hunted for fossils and ancient bones. They were learning about the past by studying modern animals and early humans.

Dr. Louis Leakey

Jane went to see Dr. Leakey. During that first visit, he asked Jane questions about African animals. He was impressed with all that she knew. Dr. Leakey hired Jane on the spot to be his secretary.

Jane loved working for the Leakeys. She learned much from them, and their study of early humans fascinated her. But she still wanted to work with living African animals.

Shortly after she was hired, Jane traveled with the Leakeys to a "dig" in Kenya. The Leakeys went to the dig to look for fossils, and they had asked her to help. During the first night out on the dig, Jane noticed the true beauty of Africa. "As we sat around our campfire that evening, I heard the distant roar of a lion," Jane recalls. "And later, as I lay on my little cot, I heard the strange, high-pitched sound I later learned was the 'giggling' of hyenas. I had never been so happy. There I was, far, far from any human dwellings, out in the wilds of Africa, with animals all around me in the night. Wild, free animals. That was what I had dreamed of all my life."

Dr. Leakey had become interested in chimpanzees. He asked Jane to go to Gombe (GAHM bee) National

Louis and Mary
Leakey on a dig

Park in Tanzania (tan zuh NEE uh) to learn all that she could about chimps. Jane was thrilled by Leakey's offer. The offer would change her life.

Other scientists doubted that Jane could do the job. She was young and female and had no formal training as a scientist. On the other hand, Leakey knew that Jane wanted to live among the apes. He also knew that she was **industrious**. Leakey believed Jane was the right person for the job. In the end, Jane and Dr. Leakey agreed that she would study chimpanzees.

13

Jane went back to England to study and prepare for her trip. She read everything she could about chimps. She took a job at the London Zoo so that she could watch chimps every day. And she waited to go back to Africa.

CHAPTER 3

The Research Begins

Jane was eager to get back to Africa, but she had to wait. First Dr. Leakey had to find money to pay for Jane's chimp study. He was only able to find enough money to pay for six months of research.

The government of Tanzania thought that being alone in Africa's wild places was dangerous for a young woman. They would not allow Jane to go to Gombe National Park by herself, so Jane asked her mother to join her. Her mother was excited by the offer. She was happy to help her daughter with her project.

Jane and her mother gathered supplies for their stay in Africa. Because Gombe had no stores, they had to pack everything they would need. They packed tents and canned food. They also packed many notebooks for Jane to use. They packed plain-colored clothing that would help them blend in with the forest.

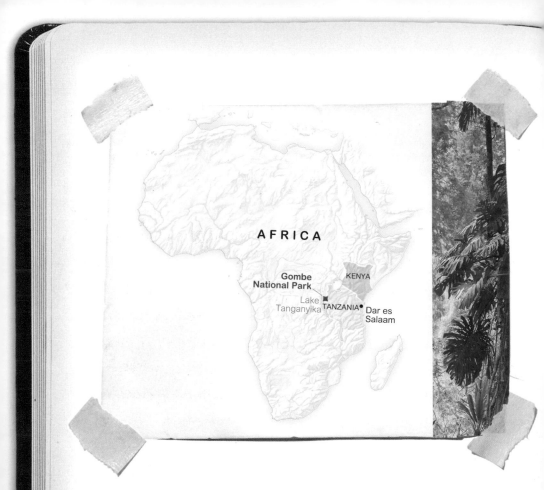

When Jane and her mother finally arrived in Tanzania, they loaded their supplies into a small boat. An African guide took them up Lake Tanganyika (tan guhn YEE kuh) to Gombe National Park. Jane was 26 years old when she landed on that **remote** sandy shore. She had no idea that she would study chimpanzees in Gombe for more than 20 years.

Jane's first evening in Gombe was magical. As she recalls, "I remember sitting on a rock, looking out over the valley and up into the blue sky, and hoping that this is what it might be like in heaven. I met some baboons, who barked at me. I heard a variety of birds. I breathed in the smell of sun-dried grass, the dry earth, and the heady scent of some kind of ripe fruit. . . . By the time I lay down to sleep on my camp bed under the twinkling stars, I already felt that I belonged in this new forest world, that this was where I was meant to be."

Gombe had many wild animals. Gombe's game warden was in charge of all the animals and visitors there. He would not let Jane hike alone because he was afraid for her safety. When Jane left camp each day to look for chimps, she had to take at least one African scout with her. Jane was not happy about this rule. Two or more hikers made more noise than one. Their noise scared away the chimps before Jane could see them well.

Jane faced many challenges in her first months in Gombe. She knew that her project would end if she did not quickly learn something about chimps. Jane and the scouts hiked in the forest every day.

The chimps ran away every time Jane and the scouts came close. Then Jane and her mother became ill. They both had very high fevers. Jane's mother became so weak that she almost died. They both recovered, but time was running out!

The game warden finally let Jane hike alone. She began to hike quietly in the forest for hours. Being alone allowed her to learn about the chimps. Using binoculars, she watched the chimps and learned about their way of life. She found a mountain that gave her a fine view of two different valleys. She also climbed trees to watch the chimps.

Jane found that about fifty chimps lived near the camp. From them she learned that chimps like to spend their days in small groups. Each group contains two or three males or a mother and her young. These smaller groups often join other chimp groups. When groups get together, they make a lot of noise. Jane also learned that when the chimps are ready to go to sleep at night, they climb a tree and look for a fork in the tree's large branches. Then they make a sleeping nest by weaving small branches together. Jane also saw that the chimps use leafy twigs to make pillows for their head.

Jane **persevered** and was able to learn much more. She studied the chimps silently day after day. Slowly the chimps grew used to seeing her. But they still ran away when she got close.

Jane taking notes on the Gombe chimps

CHAPTER 4

Exciting Discoveries

Each morning, Jane awoke at 5:30 and ate a small breakfast. Then she hiked up the mountain before the sun came up. All day she watched the chimps through her binoculars. Quietly she moved closer to the chimps, hoping they would not run away. At sunset she hiked back to camp for supper. Sometimes she went back up the mountain after supper to sleep near a chimp's nest. Then she was able to watch the chimps wake up in the morning. On other evenings, she stayed in camp to write notes about what she had seen that day. Jane kept careful notes on each chimp's **behavior**. She soon realized that each chimp had its own look and personality. When she could recognize each chimp, she gave each one a name.

Jane's mother set up a clinic for local people who were sick. It turned out that the clinic also helped Jane. It helped the local people realize that the Goodalls were not there to hurt them or the animals. Eventually

Jane's mother returned to England. By then the local people trusted Jane and were helping her in any way that they could.

One day Jane watched a chimp that she had named David Graybeard. David hunted and killed a small animal. Jane watched him eat the animal and share his kill with other chimps. Jane had made an important discovery. Before that time scientists did not know that chimps knew how to hunt. They also believed that chimps did not eat meat.

Jane's mother at the clinic she set up

Soon something else surprising happened. David Graybeard visited Jane's camp! First he climbed a palm tree just outside camp. Then he came right into camp and ate a banana that had been left on a table. David Graybeard came back to camp day after day. He soon took a banana right out of Jane's

Jane with David Graybeard

hand. Before long, other chimps were joining David Graybeard on his camp visits. With David Graybeard leading the way, most chimps began to relax around Jane. Her **patience** had finally paid off. She was finally able get as close to the chimps as she wanted.

David Graybeard also provided Jane with her most exciting discovery. One morning, Jane came upon David squatting on a termite mound. She saw him pick up a blade of grass, poke the grass into a hole in the mound, and then pull it out. The grass was covered with termites. David picked the termites off with his lips and ate them.

David fished for termites again and again. When his piece of grass bent, he dropped it. Then he picked up a little twig, stripped the leaves off, and used that to fish for termites.

David had used the blade of grass as a tool! He had also made a tool from the twig. These were important discoveries. Before that time, scientists thought that only humans knew how to use and make tools. Jane quickly sent word to Dr. Leakey, who was also excited by the discovery.

Gombe chimps using sticks to fish for termites

The news of Jane's discoveries soon spread around the world. The National Geographic Society agreed to pay for Jane's study of chimpanzees. They sent a photographer named Hugo van Lawick to take pictures of Jane and the chimps. Hugo put out bananas to encourage the chimps to come close.

Although most of the chimps had become comfortable near Jane, some of the male chimps had not. One time a number of males gathered around Jane. They glared at her and made loud, threatening sounds. Jane stayed calm and close to the ground. Finally the chimps went away. Jane knew that the chimps could have really hurt her. But Jane was **courageous**. She continued with her work.

After some time Dr. Leakey felt that Jane needed more education to continue her work. Jane went back to England for awhile to study animal behavior. She studied at a university until she earned the title of Dr. Goodall.

Some chimps became very special to Jane. Flo, a chimp with ragged ears and a big nose, was one of her favorites. Flo and her young visited camp for many years. By watching Flo, Jane learned that chimp mothers take very good care of their young. She saw that female chimps usually have one baby every five or six years. She learned that chimp family members help one another throughout their whole life.

Jane Goodall and Hugo van Lawick shared a love of animals and nature. Hugo took many wonderful photos of the chimps of Gombe. Many magazines published his photos. The news of Jane's discoveries, along with Hugo's pictures, continued to spread around the world. Jane and Hugo fell in love and were married in 1964.

Jane with Hugo van Lawick

CHAPTER 5

Gombe Becomes a Research Center

Over time the chimps at Gombe had learned to relax around people. It was then possible to be close to many of the chimps and learn about their life. Jane could not keep up. Local people and students from around the world began to help Jane with her research. Simple houses and a kitchen were built to make the researchers more comfortable. The quiet camp had become a busy research center.

Janc and the researchers learned much more. They learned that chimps use **gestures** to communicate. Chimps hug, kiss, hold hands, and pat one another on the back. These gestures appear to mean almost the same thing to chimps as they do to humans. The research team also learned that chimps use different calls to communicate to each other. Chimps do not talk as people do. They use about thirty different calls to send messages to one another. If a chimp is afraid, it calls out loudly. Even chimps who are far away rush to the calling chimp to find out what is going on.

Something else the researchers noticed was that chimps spend a lot of time close to their friends. They spend a lot of time sitting close together and grooming each other. Chimps groom each other for many reasons. Grooming clears a friend's skin and calms a nervous chimp. It also calms a restless baby chimp.

Jane watching chimps groom each other

Jane and the researchers also saw that chimps love to play. Chimps often tickle one another. They spend a lot of time wrestling and chasing their friends, too.

In 1967 Jane gave birth to a son, Hugo, who was later nicknamed Grub. Jane wanted to spend as much time as possible with her new baby. She continued to live at Gombe, but she no longer spent her days in the forest, watching the chimps. Each day Jane checked on the researchers to find out what they were learning. She missed watching the chimps, but she loved watching her son grow up.

Jane and Grub at Gombe

Grub spent his early life outdoors with an adult close to him. Grub loved to play on the beach and in the water. He learned to swim when he was very young. When Grub was older, his parents hired a teacher to come to Gombe.

Hugo's work as a photographer took him all over the world. Jane felt it was important to continue her work at Gombe. The couple began to grow apart. Jane and Hugo divorced when Grub was seven. Jane wished that her marriage had worked out differently. But she and Hugo remained good friends.

About a year later, Jane married a man named Derek Bryceson. Derek had lived in Africa for a long time, and he was the director of Tanzania's National Parks. Derek helped Jane as her research center grew.

After Jane married Derek Bryceson, she spent much of her time at his home in Dar es Salaam, Tanzania. She went there to write a book about her research. While Jane was away, the researchers continued their work. They followed the chimps up steep mountain slopes and through the thick forest. They often could predict which way the chimps would go. They could also keep up with a chimp who swung quickly from tree to tree.

Jane had always believed that chimps were kind and gentle creatures. During her first years in Gombe, she saw that most of the chimps got along with each other most of the time. In 1972 her ideas began to change. Jane and the rest of the researchers began to see fighting between male chimps. These chimps were fighting over who was going to stay in that place. Some chimps no longer wanted other chimps to be in their area. This fighting among the chimps lasted for four years. The unwanted chimps left to form their own group. Jane came to understand that chimps have both good and bad sides.

Jane and Derek had been married for only a few years when Derek became very ill. He died in 1980. His death was very difficult for Jane. After Derek died, Jane went back to Gombe. She walked in the forest and spent time with the

Jane and Derek Bryceson

chimps. Being in the company of the chimps and in the beautiful forest helped Jane. She began to regain her spirit after the loss of her beloved husband.

Jane with young chimps

CHAPTER 6

The Time to Teach

Jane's book *The Chimpanzees of Gombe* was published in 1986. The book recorded what she had learned during her 25-year study of chimps. Jane began traveling to talk about her book. During her travels she learned that animals all across Africa needed help.

When Jane first went to Gombe in 1960, about 10,000 chimps lived in Tanzania. By 1990 only about 2500 were left. People were cutting down forests for farms and houses. Wild animals had fewer places to live. Chimps and other wild animals were being hunted for meat or sold as pets. The number of wild animals living in Africa was quickly dropping.

Jane also saw that many people in Africa also needed help. Jane felt that we are all **responsible** for the lives of African people and animals. It was time for her life to change. Jane made a promise to teach people about the problems in Africa. She now travels most of the time.

She spends only a few weeks a year at Gombe. Jane does not always enjoy living out of a suitcase. But she is happy that her travels have allowed her to meet wonderful people around the world. Jane continues to work with others to find ways to **protect** chimpanzees and other animals. She talks with leaders of different countries to find ways to protect all wild animals.

The work at Gombe goes on because of the **dedicated** Tanzanian researchers. They are still learning new things about chimps. Recently they saw that a mother chimp had given birth to twins. This is only the third time in 40 years that twin chimps have been seen!

Jane has worked hard to stop the hunting and selling of chimps. She has helped set up sanctuaries (SANG choo air eez) for chimps. Sanctuaries are safe places for animals to live.

Jane with a chimp at a sanctuary

In sanctuaries chimps are cared for and can live safely for the rest of their life.

Because chimps have bodies similar to human bodies, scientists have used chimps to test new drugs for many years. Jane visited laboratories where scientists keep these chimps. She found that chimps were often kept alone in small, dark cages.

Seeing chimps living in such gloomy places upset Jane, but she did not get angry with the laboratory researchers. Instead, she told the researchers stories. She told them about David Graybeard, who loved to climb and play. She spoke of Flo, who took such good care of her young. Her stories **persuaded** the researchers to treat chimps better so that the chimps can have better lives.

Jane believes that finding cures for human diseases is important. She works with researchers to help them find cures without using animals. She hopes that one day soon, no animals will be needed for any kind of research.

Jane wants animals in zoos to have more room to move around and play. She works with zoos around the world to help them make their zoos more **humane** for the animals in their care.

Jane believes it is important to teach children to care for the earth and for one another. She believes that young people can make the world a better place. Jane started the Roots & Shoots program to teach young people ways to become **humanitarians**. Through Roots & Shoots, children learn how to take care of the earth and its living creatures.

Jane teaches children simple ways to make a difference in the world. She asks children to do things such as turning off the water while they brush their teeth. She also asks them to pick up litter and to turn off lights when leaving a room.

Jane talking with children about Roots & Shoots

She **encourages** children to be kind to the people and animals around them.

Jane tells children everywhere, "You can make a difference! You get to choose: Do you want to use your life to try to make the world a better place for humans and animals and the environment? Or not?"

Jane has many plans for the future. She hopes to spend more time with her son, Grub, and his family. But she does not plan to stop working any time soon. Although she is no longer young, Jane feels she has been blessed with very good health. She plans to continue traveling and teaching as long as she is able. Jane feels she still has work to do.

To find out more about Jane Goodall or Roots & Shoots, visit her Web site at www.janegoodall.org.

Timeline of Jane Goodall's Life

1934	*Jane Goodall is born on April 3.*
1939	*World War II begins.*
1952	*Jane trains as a secretary.*
1957	*Jane sails to Africa for the first time.*
1957	*Jane begins working for Louis and Mary Leakey.*
1960	*Jane begins her work at the Gombe National Park in Tanzania.*
1961	*Jane makes important discoveries about chimpanzee behavior.*
1964	*Jane marries Hugo van Lawick.*
1965	*The National Geographic Society begins to fund Jane's work.*
1967	*Jane and Hugo have a son, Grub.*
1975	*Jane marries Derek Bryceson.* *Jane founds the Jane Goodall Institute for Research, Education, and Conservation.*
1980	*Derek Bryceson dies.*
1984	*Jane wins the J. Paul Getty Wildlife Conservation Prize.*
1986	*Jane publishes* The Chimpanzees of Gombe. *Jane wins the American Society for Prevention of Cruelty to Animals award for humane excellence.*
1991	*Jane begins Roots & Shoots.*
2000	*Jane serves as the National Geographic Society's Explorer-in-Residence.*

GLOSSARY

behavior (bih HAYV yuhr) a person's or animal's actions

compassion (kuhm PASH uhn) sadness about the troubles of another

courageous (kuh RAY juhs) brave

dedicated (DED uh kay tid) devoted to one's work

determined (duh TUHR mind) having one's mind made up; showing a strong will

donations (doh NAY shunz) gifts or amounts of money

encourages (ehn KUHR ij iz) gives hope or courage to someone

excelled (ik SELD) did better than another person

gestures (JES chuhrz) body movements used to communicate

grateful (GRAYT fuhl) feeling thankful

humane (hyoo MAYN) kind, tender, merciful

humanitarians (hyoo man ih TAYR ee uhnz) people who try to improve the lives of humans

independent (ihn dih PEN duhnt) earning one's own living

industrious (ihn DUHS tree uhs) hardworking

patience (PAY shuhnts) the ability to wait calmly for something or to deal with problems calmly

persevered (puhr suh VEERD) continued with some effort

persuaded (puhr SWAY did) made another person do or believe something; convinced

protect (pruh TEKT) to keep from injury or loss

remote (rih MOHT) far off or hidden away

responsible (rih SPAHN suh buhl) taking on a duty or having a sense of duty

thrifty (THRIF tee) careful in the use of money

understanding (uhn duhr STAND ing) showing kindness

INDEX